ONLINE SHAMING AND BULLYING

BY TAMMY GAGNE

INTOLERANCE AND VIOLENCE IN SOCIETY

ReferencePoint Press®

San Diego, CA

© 2020 ReferencePoint Press, Inc.
Printed in the United States

For more information, contact:
ReferencePoint Press, Inc.
PO Box 27779
San Diego, CA 92198
www.ReferencePointPress.com

ALL RIGHTS RESERVED.

No part of this work covered by the copyright hereon may be reproduced or used in any form or by any means—graphic, electronic, or mechanical, including photocopying, recording, taping, web distribution, or information storage retrieval systems—without the written permission of the publisher.

LIBRARY OF CONGRESS CATALOGING-IN-PUBLICATION DATA

Names: Gagne, Tammy, author.
Title: Online shaming and bullying / by Tammy Gagne.
Description: San Diego, CA : ReferencePoint Press, Inc., [2020] | Series: Intolerance and violence in society | Audience: Grade 9 to 12. | Includes bibliographical references and index.
Identifiers: LCCN 2019003301 (print) | LCCN 2019006561 (ebook) | ISBN 9781682826881 (ebook) | ISBN 9781682826874 (hardcover)
Subjects: LCSH: Cyberbullying. | Shame.
Classification: LCC HV6773.15.C92 (ebook) | LCC HV6773.15.C92 G34 2020 (print) | DDC 302.34/302854678--dc23
LC record available at https://lccn.loc.gov/2019003301

CONTENTS

Important Events in the History
of Intolerance and Violence ... 4

INTRODUCTION
Bullying and Shaming Today ... 6

CHAPTER ONE
How Did Online Shaming
and Bullying Begin? ... 10

CHAPTER TWO
How Can People Recognize
Online Shaming and Bullying? ... 24

CHAPTER THREE
What Groups Are Most Often
Targets of Online Shaming and Bullying? ... 38

CHAPTER FOUR
How Can Society Prevent
Online Shaming and Bullying? ... 54

Source Notes ... 70
For Further Research ... 74
Index ... 76
Image Credits ... 79
About the Author ... 80

IMPORTANT EVENTS IN THE HISTORY OF
INTOLERANCE AND VIOLENCE

2006
Megan Meier kills herself after the mother of a former friend creates a MySpace page under the fake name of Josh Evans, bullying Megan through this false persona.

2008
Jessica Logan kills herself after an ex-boyfriend shares nude photos of her with others who begin bullying her. Logan's parents file a lawsuit against the Montgomery, Ohio, school district, which eventually leads to the Jessica Logan Act, a state anti-bullying law.

1999
Georgia becomes the first state to enact anti-bullying laws.

1999 2006 2007 2008 2010

1999
Columbine High School students Eric Harris and Dylan Klebold open fire on their classmates in one of the worst school shootings in US history; news reports state that the two had been bullied.

2007
Smartphones begin to dramatically increase in popularity. These devices make it easier for people to communicate, but they also make it easier to bully people.

2010
Rutgers University student Tyler Clementi jumps to his death from the George Washington Bridge after his college roommate circulates a video of him kissing another man.

2016
Olympic gymnast Gabby Douglas speaks publicly about being bullied online for her appearance.

2018
Nine-year-old Jamel Myles kills himself in Denver, Colorado, after being bullied at school for coming out as gay.

2014
Art student Lindsay Bottos turns bullying comments she receives into art with her "Anonymous" photo series on Tumblr.

2014   2015   2016   2017   2018

2015
Minnesota dentist Walter Palmer faces online shaming for killing Cecil the Lion, a popular animal at Hwange National Park in Zimbabwe.

2017
US First Lady Melania Trump unveils her "Be Best" initiative that discourages negative behaviors including bullying.

2016
The Duke and Duchess of Cambridge create the Royal Foundation Taskforce on the Prevention of Cyberbullying to help fight online bullying.

INTRODUCTION

BULLYING AND SHAMING TODAY

Leia Pierce was driving with her children to her mother's home in the summer of 2018 when her nine-year-old son, Jamel Myles, made a sudden announcement. "I'm gay," he told his mother and two sisters.[1] Although his mother was surprised by the spontaneous nature of her son's statement, she focused on supporting him. She responded simply by assuring him that she still loved him. The two had a close relationship. This had likely helped Jamel when he had been bullied at school the previous year.

But the bullying continued when he returned to school that August, and it intensified when Jamel decided to come out as gay to his classmates at Joe Shoemaker Elementary School in Denver, Colorado. Overwhelmed by the harassment, Jamel took his own life by hanging himself in his bedroom closet after his fourth day of fourth grade. "Those bullies are the reason my son's not with me," Pierce told NBC News following her son's death. "My daughter told me, he came home and told her kids at school were telling him to kill himself."[2]

Sadly, Jamel is just one of many children who have died by suicide in recent years after being bullied by their peers. In 2017, twelve-year-old Mallory Grossman of Rockaway, New Jersey, took her own life after being bullied through text messages and online posts. Bullying-driven suicide is not just happening in the United States. In Japan in 2016, thirteen-year-old Rima Kasai killed herself

Kids are often bullied at school. Bullying can be hard for kids to handle.

and left behind a message on her smartphone that she couldn't stand being bullied any longer. Costas Yannopoulos is the president of the European Anti-Bullying Network. In a statement by the group, he said, "When a child tries to commit suicide because of bullying it means that this is a serious issue within our society which is developing into a public health issue."[3]

A WIDESPREAD PROBLEM

The problem of online shaming and bullying has reached unprecedented levels, infiltrating all areas of life for both adults and children. Social media has made it especially easy for bullies to target their victims, expanding the reach and audience for public shaming. While bullying is nothing new, the constant presence of the internet

> "When a child tries to commit suicide because of bullying it means that this is a serious issue within our society which is developing into a public health issue."³
>
> – Costas Yannopoulos, president of the European Anti-Bullying Network, 2015

has made it impossible for victims to escape the abuse.

Rarely is bullying an isolated incident. Instead, it is an ongoing attack. Bullying may take place in person with physical assaults. Or the attacks may be verbal. In this case, victims might be publicly humiliated by name-calling either in person or online. They might be the subject of rumors or be excluded socially by the bully and all of his or her friends. Although many bullies are children, the behavior doesn't stop when they grow up. In a 2015 article in the *New Yorker*, writer Maria Konnikova stated, "Workplace and professional bullying is just as common as childhood bullying; often, it's just less obvious."⁴

As studies provide more information about why and to whom bullying is occurring, parents, teachers, and bosses, along with school counselors, social workers, and psychologists, are all trying to find strategies for dealing with the problem. Stopping it before it causes irreparable damage for the victim is paramount. Finding ways to prevent bullying before it occurs is also a common goal.

Research has identified behaviors that often precede bullying with kids—including laughing at others, name-calling, and excluding certain kids from social activities. Susan Patterson, who leads a cyberbullying course at Lesley University in Cambridge, Massachusetts, elaborated, "The research would imply that [these behaviors] lead to bullying, and that if we can stop kids [from doing those behaviors], then we're going to go a long way to stopping the problem."⁵

Most teens have access to social media and cell phones. This extends bullies' abilities to pursue their victims.

BULLYING AND SHAMING TODAY

With technology expanding the ways that people can communicate with one another, bullying continues to provide new challenges for those seeking to end it. Many experts say that this behavior will never completely end, but others are hopeful that simply reducing it wherever possible will make a meaningful difference. It isn't just adults who want to take part in that process. Kids want to find solutions too. In an article for BullyingEducation.org, author MaryAnn Byrne wrote,

> We hear a great many platitudes these days about 'taking a stand against bullying.' I believe that most of these people are honest. They do wish the best for the youth of America and do want bullying behaviors to cease. The problem is that everyone wants a quick fix. There is no quick fix. It takes time. Kids did not learn how to bully overnight and they will not unlearn it overnight. But they do want to learn."[6]

CHAPTER ONE

HOW DID ONLINE SHAMING AND BULLYING BEGIN?

Shaming and bullying are problems at least as old as human society itself, but in recent decades they have become considerably larger issues. A few decades ago, the word *bully* may have evoked an image of a physically imposing schoolyard tormentor picking on a smaller or less popular child. Bullies were also sometimes seen in the workplace, keeping other employees from advancing up the corporate ladder through tactics including threats and other forms of intimidation. While those forms of bullying still exist, advances in technology have brought bullying to virtual platforms as well, with the internet intensifying the impact of this behavior. Cyberbullying can often have offline consequences, sometimes devastating ones. Many victims of online shaming and bullying suffer from intense depression. Some cases of online bullying have resulted in the victims attempting suicide. Others who are bullied become part of an abusive cycle by becoming bullies themselves.

According to a 2018 survey by the Pew Research Center, 59 percent of teenagers in the United States reported suffering from some type of bullying online. An even higher percentage of teens said that cyberbullying has become a major problem for today's youth. Kids who spend the most time online face the highest risk of being

Bullies often physically intimidate others. However, bullying can take many forms.

bullied. This is striking in light of the report's findings that 45 percent of teens reported being online "almost constantly."[7] Bullies learn quickly that the internet can be used as a powerful tool in hurting and manipulating others.

Scott Poland, a professor at the Center for Psychological Studies at Nova Southeastern University in Florida, points out that the internet has significantly changed the dynamics involved in many bullying situations. He explains,

When I was a kid, once you got home your house was the safe haven. No one could reach you. . . . But today with the advent of all the technology it's like the home is not necessarily a safe

> **"Perhaps one third of all adolescent girls wake up in the middle of the night to check and see what might have been posted about them."** [8]
>
> – Professor Scott Poland, 2018

haven after all. There is some literature indicating that perhaps one third of all adolescent girls wake up in the middle of the night to check and see what might have been posted about them. I think we have to recognize that the impact of it is really quite severe.[8]

In many cases bullies target people close to their own age. However, the behavior of adults can often influence the way kids choose to act toward others. In 2006, a thirteen-year-old girl named Megan Meier began an online friendship with a sixteen-year-old boy named Josh Evans through MySpace, a predecessor to more modern social media services such as Facebook and Instagram. Meier had a crush on Evans and enjoyed their online conversations, which had developed into what appeared to be a romantic relationship. But nothing about the situation was what it appeared to be.

One day when Megan logged on to her MySpace account, she received a message from Josh stating that he no longer wanted to be friends with her. He claimed that he had heard she did not treat her friends well and that he did not want to associate with someone so mean. Megan was hurt and did not understand who had said these things about her. Before she could get to the bottom of the situation, it got even worse. She began seeing public messages on the website which called her a variety of derogatory names, attacked her appearance, and accused her of being sexually promiscuous.

Teens need to be safe when talking to strangers on social media. Parents often place restrictions on kids' social media time or interactions.

The final message she received from this boy she had come to care about stated, "The world would be a better place without you."[9]

Shortly after that, Megan's parents instructed her to log off from the computer. They told her that anyone who could say such things clearly did not know her. Devastated by the hateful words being hurled at her so publicly online, Megan ran to her bedroom. Her parents tried to figure out how to handle the situation while they made dinner for their family. Before the meal was fully prepared, however, Megan had already taken drastic measures in response to the online bullying. She decided to end her own life by hanging herself inside her closet.

Megan's parents told the police what had transpired online earlier in the day between their daughter and Josh. The family was already devastated by Megan's death, but at this point they only knew part of what had actually happened to her. As the Federal Bureau of Investigation (FBI) began investigating the case, the story became even more complicated. Josh Evans had never existed. His MySpace account had been created by Lori Drew, the mother of one of Megan's former friends, after the teens experienced a falling out. Mutual friends told the Meiers that Drew created Josh with the intention of seeking revenge against Megan. Not only was Megan tormented to the point of suicide, but she had apparently been the victim of a bully who was forty-seven years old.

Drew faced multiple charges following Megan's death, but none led to a conviction. She was acquitted of the felony charges of intentionally causing harm while accessing computers without authorization. Later, a judge also threw out her convictions on lesser charges of computer fraud. Although the Meiers do not think Drew or her daughter intended for Megan to end her life, both Ron and Tina Meier hold Lori Drew responsible for their daughter's suicide. In an interview with ABC News, Tina Meier said, "She played a ridiculous game with my daughter's life."[10]

SMARTPHONES AS WEAPONS

The internet had created an efficient means for bullies to target their victims, but technology's role in the problem would soon grow as new devices increased the reach of online shaming and bullying. In 2007, less than a year after Megan Meier's death, Apple introduced its first smartphone, the iPhone. Smartphones enabled people to access the internet, send emails and text messages, and easily connect with social networking services. At first it was mostly adults who owned these expensive yet remarkably convenient devices, but they

Embarrassing or private photos can be humiliating for teens if they are shared. Once they are shared, they can be hard to stop.

gradually became indispensable tech gear for young people as well. Whereas kids had previously needed to log on to desktop computers to access social media, they could now post messages and photos anytime, anywhere.

In 2008, eighteen-year-old Jessica Logan used her smartphone to send nude photos of herself to her then-boyfriend. Shortly after the couple broke up, he decided to text the images to other girls, who then shared them with other students. Many of the teens reacted to the photos by harassing Jessica. They messaged her relentlessly, calling her horrible names. Jessica's mother, Cynthia Logan, realized that something was wrong when the attendance office at Sycamore High School in Montgomery, Ohio, contacted her to say that Jessica was skipping classes repeatedly. It took Cynthia Logan a while to get to the bottom of the problem, but she ultimately learned that her daughter was avoiding school because of online shaming and bullying over the photos, which other students were continuing to circulate. "She was being attacked and tortured," her mother told *Today* in 2016.[11]

Other students witnessed the ordeal as it was unfolding. Jessica's friend Lauren Taylor told NBC News, "When she would come to school, she would always hear, 'Oh, that's the girl who sent the picture.'"[12] Taylor said that the students would then belittle Jessica by calling her names.

Cynthia Logan claimed that the school was also aware of the problem, and that officials there did little to stop the bullying. After enduring two months of this treatment, Jessica decided to end her life to escape the harassment. Her parents thought that if the school would have done more to stop the situation, it might have prevented their daughter from taking her life. For this reason, the Logans filed a lawsuit against the school district. Although the case would take multiple years, it ended with a $154,000 settlement for the Logans because of the school's failure to protect Jessica from the sexual harassment she received. The lawsuit also led to a state law called the Jessica Logan Act, which requires schools to take steps toward preventing online bullying and to provide teachers with anti-bullying training.

The statistics relating to bullying are more severe than many people might imagine. According to a study conducted in the United Kingdom, at least one-half of the suicides of young people today involve some type of bullying. The numbers from other studies are equally discouraging. Yale University has found that victims of bullies are up to nine times more likely to consider taking their own lives than

BULLYING AND SELF-HARM

There is a strong link between bullying and self-harm among children. When kids between the ages of five and twelve years old are bullied, their likelihood of hurting themselves triples compared with kids who have not experienced bullying. The risks increase as kids get older. Children who are bullied in elementary school are five times more likely to harm themselves as teenagers.

Self-harm does not always begin with thoughts of suicide. Many times behaviors such as cutting, burning, or hitting develop long before thoughts of ending one's life enter the equation. If anyone notices anyone engaging in self-harm, the behavior should be addressed, as this is a serious situation in itself. Although self-harm is not always caused by bullying, noticing these behaviors can help identify a bullying problem before it leads to more serious self-harm. It is estimated that eliminating bullying could prevent as many as 20 percent of all self-harm cases.

---

kids who have not been bullied. To make matters even worse, many families do not see any justice after losing a child to online bullying.

Thirteen-year-old Hope Witsell also was a victim of online shaming after sending a naked photo of herself to a boyfriend. The image then ended up in the hands of another girl, who sent the image to students at six other schools in the Florida area where the kids lived. Hope's bullies created an online site about her, calling it the "Hope Hater Page."

Like Jessica Logan, Hope was distraught over the online bullying she was receiving. After a while, her mental condition started to concern her school's social worker, who asked Hope to sign a contract promising not to harm herself. No matter how well-intended this agreement was, it did nothing to save the young girl's life. Hope's mother later found her dead in her bedroom. Knowing nothing of the contract until she found it in Hope's bedroom wastebasket, Donna Witsell was amazed that the school had not shared its concerns with her.

Officials at Shields Middle School claimed that the social worker had tried to get in touch with Hope's parents, but Donna Witsell did not believe this was true. As she explained to CNN, "The school did not call. We have the digital telephone; we have the cell phones that indicate when there was an incoming call and what number was calling in. We have a house phone, I have a cell phone, my husband has a cell phone. We have emergency contact numbers at the school which was my sister-in-law and her husband. There was no indication that the school called any of those numbers."[13]

Although Hope's parents filed two lawsuits against the school for wrongful death, both suits were ultimately dismissed. This result did not stop Donna Witsell from speaking out about her daughter's online bullying—or from trying to prevent it from happening to other kids. Through an anti-bullying organization called Triangle Resolutions, she helps other young people get counseling to cope with shaming and bullying. In an interview with the *Tampa Bay Times*, Donna Witsell said, "Every time I see or I hear about another child committing suicide, I scream inside. I want to know when it is going to stop. People need to get an

"**People need to get an awareness. They need to see the reality and what these kids are going through.**"[14]

– *Donna Witsell, parent of a bullying victim*

awareness. They need to see the reality and what these kids are going through."[14]

TARGETED FOR THEIR DIFFERENCES

According to an article in *Health Science Journal*, victims of online bullying are most often targeted for the ways in which they may be different from their peers, including "race, religion, culture, sexual orientation, physical ability and features, intellectual ability, social status, and personality."[15] While this list is long and varied, it offers some insight into how bullying can be prevented. One of the biggest factors in preventing this problem is creating and maintaining empathy among young people. Mentally healthy individuals who feel empathy and tolerance for people different from themselves are far less likely to bully others.

In addition to affecting victims' mental health, bullying can also have a negative impact on their education. Lisa M. Williams, a doctoral student in sociology at Ohio State University, conducted a study on how bullying affects students' academic success. In an interview with NEA Today, Williams shared, "Although academic achievement is largely influenced by family background and school characteristics, our study suggests that the experience of being bullied also influences students' grades. We find that bullying has implications for achievement regardless of racial and ethnic background, but seems to be especially detrimental for subsets of certain racial and ethnic groups."[16] Black and Latino students who had GPAs of 3.5 in the ninth grade and were bullied the following year saw a drop in their GPAs of between 0.3 and 0.5 points by the time they got to twelfth grade.

When a person's sexual orientation or gender identity is targeted by bullies, it can be profoundly hurtful. Members of the LGBT (lesbian, gay, bisexual, and transgender) community, for example, go through different timelines of readiness to share their identities with the rest of the world. While some people are eager to come out, many people need time to prepare for this process or simply prefer to reveal their identities more gradually. When a bully outs an LGBT person, it can be an especially traumatic experience for the victim.

This type of incident can be worsened when technology gives a bully the ability to amplify their harassment. Tyler Clementi was a freshman at Rutgers University in 2010 when his roommate set up a video camera in their dorm room without Clementi's knowledge. Suspecting that Clementi was gay, Dharun Ravi recorded a video of Clementi kissing another man. He then tweeted about what he had seen and shared the video with other students. Clementi was so distressed over the incident that he killed himself by jumping off the George Washington Bridge three days later.

Ravi was charged and convicted for invasion of privacy and fourteen other counts relating to the incident. In 2016, however, a New Jersey appeals court threw out the conviction. In response to the court's decision, Clementi's parents issued a statement. It read in part, "We know that Tyler's private moments were stolen from him and used to humiliate him. His life was forever affected and the lives of those who knew and loved him have been forever changed. In light of today's decision, we will do what we encourage all people to do before they push that send button, and that is to pause and consider the implications of their message. Does it encourage and build someone up or does it destroy and harm another person?"[17]

Following his death, Clementi's parents founded the Tyler Clementi Foundation, which works to educate people about the dangers of bullying and protect young LGBT people from being harassed.

Following Tyler Clementi's suicide, his parents set up a foundation in his name. The Tyler Clementi Foundation works to protect LGBT youth from bullying like Tyler Clementi faced.

The foundation works with students from middle school through college. As part of their efforts, the Clementis have urged federal legislators to pass a bill with their son's name—the Tyler Clementi Higher Education Anti-Harassment Act.

In 2016, Clementi's mother, Jane Clementi, submitted written testimony to the Senate Health, Education, Labor, and Pensions (HELP) Committee, urging its members to push the bill forward. She wrote:

I believe a bill will allow institutions of higher education to take a fresh look and reexamine their policies and procedures

> "Bullying does not magically disappear when someone turns eighteen. We must continue to provide safe and supportive learning environments for all students in all learning environments including higher education."[18]
>
> – Jane Clementi, mother of bullying victim Tyler Clementi

that are and are not in place. In addition this legislation is your opportunity to not only keep your own young adults safe but to also have a global influence. Bullying does not magically disappear when someone turns eighteen. We must continue to provide safe and supportive learning environments for all students in all learning environments including higher education.[18]

The bill passed into law in 2017. It requires all colleges and universities that receive federal funding to make policies that prohibit cyberbullying. The policies also ban bullying based on perceived race, color, national origin, sex, disability, sexual orientation, gender identity, or religion.

WHEN THE BULLIED BECOME BULLIES

Some people who experience bullying respond by becoming bullies themselves. In rare cases, this has resulted in devastating violence against others. One of the first high-profile examples of this was the school shooting at Columbine High School in Littleton, Colorado. On April 20, 1999, Columbine students Eric Harris and Dylan Klebold opened fire on their classmates and teachers, killing thirteen people and wounding twenty others. As more and more incidents of mass violence have taken place in schools, the media has begun connecting the dots between bullying and the perpetrators of these crimes. Many of them have acted out in response to being harassed by their peers. In 2018, NBC News, *Newsweek*, and the *Wall Street Journal* were just a few of the news outlets that ran stories about the past bullying of school shooters. Although each case is different, data from the US Secret Service reveals that 71 percent of school shooters felt "persecuted, bullied, threatened, attacked, or injured" prior to their violent acts.[19]

On September 13, 2017, fifteen-year-old Caleb Sharpe brought a semiautomatic rifle and handgun to Freeman High School in Washington with a plan to harm his classmates. The sophomore fatally shot one student and injured three others. After he was arrested, Sharpe said that he had wanted to "teach everyone a lesson about what happens when you bully others."[20] Very few bullied kids will commit a school shooting. But with so many of the shooters sharing that they have been victims of this kind of harassment, experts stress that preventing bullying could lessen the incidence of this horrific violence.

In an article for the National Public Radio website, education blogger Anya Kamenetz addressed the link between bullying and school violence. After interviewing several experts on the topic, she explained that schools need to focus more on improving the social and emotional health of their students. In her piece, Kamenetz wrote, "If you devote resources to shutting down bullying, discrimination, and harassment, there is a chance to de-escalate conflict before it starts."[21]

> "If you devote resources to shutting down bullying, discrimination, and harassment, there is a chance to de-escalate conflict before it starts."[21]
>
> – Education blogger Anya Kamenetz, 2013

CHAPTER TWO

HOW CAN PEOPLE RECOGNIZE ONLINE SHAMING AND BULLYING?

Online shaming has become so prevalent that many people do not even recognize it when they see it or realize when they are participating in it. People who write for entertainment gossip websites or make disparaging posts about celebrities to social media hold a share of the responsibility, but without visitors, these sites would not exist. Each day millions of people log on to sites that ridicule famous people for their weight, fashion choices, and other things that modern society deems unacceptable in one way or another, and all visitors share in the responsibility of this widespread bullying.

Olympic gymnast Gabby Douglas has a large following of fans who have cheered her on as she has competed at national and international levels in her sport. With three gold medals, Douglas has become a role model for other young gymnasts. Many of them consider themselves dedicated fans, but that hasn't stopped all of them from reading stories and online posts that have shamed her over the years. The topics have varied from the way she wears her hair to how muscular her body looks.

Gabby Douglas has been in the public eye since her first Olympic appearance. This visibility often comes with unfair judgments and internet comments.

For a while the hateful comments took their toll on Douglas, who spent a lot of time crying over these stories when she was younger. At times they even made her feel like quitting. But Douglas was able to turn to a role model of her own. For her, that was tennis great Serena Williams. In 2016, Gabby's mother, Natalie Hawkins, told *People* magazine, "Gabrielle saw the elegance with which Serena Williams handled all the negative criticism of her own body. It was liberating for my daughter to see that."[22] Gabby has said that Williams helped her realize that she didn't have to apologize for her body.

Body shaming is a common problem, even for many celebrities. Actress Ariel Winter stars in the popular ABC sitcom *Modern Family*. She's also a young woman, like so many others her age, who enjoys posting selfies to social media. With so many followers, her photos often attract a lot of attention from both fans and critics. The latter have led Winter to become a vocal opponent of body shaming, capitalizing on the publicity generated by online bullies. "Every time someone bullies me online," she posted to Instagram in 2016, "it gives me a chance to [reemphasize] to my fans, and even myself, how important self-acceptance is."[23]

A healthy self-image can be a great defense against the pain that online shaming and bullying can inflict, but even people with tremendous confidence can feel hurt by public shaming. In December 2018, singer Meghan Trainor cohosted *Today with Kathie Lee and Hoda* when the program tackled the complicated topic of online shaming. Even though she is known for singing such empowering songs such as "All About That Bass" and "I Love Me," Trainor admitted that she sometimes feels the sting of mean online comments just as any other person would. "I think at the end of the day," she said, "no matter if you're a pop star or what your career is, or what age you're at, I think you'll be affected by it."[24]

> "I think at the end of the day, no matter if you're a pop star or what your career is, or what age you're at, I think you'll be affected by it."[24]
>
> – Meghan Trainor, speaking about online shaming, 2018

SHAMING PEOPLE FOR THEIR PARENTING CHOICES

Although many internet users understand that shaming people for their appearance is bullying behavior, a surprising number do not object as strongly when people are publicly criticized for their actions. Perhaps because they see actions as choices, these online critics rationalize the ridicule as a warranted consequence. This type of bullying is especially common when it comes to parenting. People often disagree about the best ways to raise children. In most cases, there is no right or wrong way to raise a child, but many people think their way is the only right way.

At one time, criticism of other people's parenting styles was limited to smaller audiences. A person might have made a snide comment to a fellow parent in passing, but most of the time people simply shared their disapproval with one or two friends more privately—or kept their opinions to themselves. Today, however, the internet has provided the critics with a larger audience.

In December 2018, actress Gabrielle Union posted a video of herself with her newborn daughter to Instagram. The video showed Union repeatedly kissing the infant, sometimes on the lips. Critics wasted no time in voicing their disapproval for Union's actions. "She's gorgeous," one fan replied, "but no kissing babies on the mouth." Another responded, "Ahhhh didn't anyone tell you you shouldn't kiss a baby in the mouth. Even your own. She's beautiful though."[25]

Other celebrities have received similar public shaming for kissing their kids on the lips. Former LA Galaxy midfielder David Beckham, New England Patriots quarterback Tom Brady, and actress and singer Hilary Duff have all become the target of online bullies after videos surfaced of them kissing their children on the mouth. Even mental health professionals have weighed in on the subject in articles about these celebrities, but as everyone shared their opinion, most people overlooked the fact that they were taking part in online shaming.

It's not just celebrities who become the victims of parent shaming. With the cell phone cameras that most people carry these days, people frequently take photos or videos of other parents in public.

Mothers often receive comments and looks in public that are meant to shame their parenting choices. Many times, the onlookers don't have the whole story.

In 2016, Molly Lensing was traveling home with her youngest daughter when they experienced a twenty-hour delay at a Colorado airport. After holding the baby in her arms for multiple hours, the young mother placed her daughter on a blanket she had spread over the floor in front of her. While Lensing was looking at her own cell phone, another person in the airport snapped a photo. When the stranger posted the image online, it went viral. Commenters immediately began sharing their disapproval, implying that Lensing was a bad mother for setting her baby on the floor.

Again, the issue was not whether this mother had made a good or bad decision, but rather how people on the internet responded to the situation. Suddenly, the photo of this mother of three, who worked part-time as a pediatric nurse, was being sent all over the world as strangers shamed her for her parenting choice in the middle of a difficult situation. In a 2017 interview with *Today*, she said that she felt her privacy was violated. "I had recently started working on a labor floor, and I was terrified of my coworkers or boss seeing the photo

SHAMING BUSINESSES

In July 2018, one company used the internet to shame another company in hopes of benefitting from the situation. The media had learned that the high-end fashion company Burberry had burned $37 million worth of unsold clothes the previous year instead of discounting the clothing or donating it to charity. Another company, thredUp—an online secondhand clothing business—was appalled at Burberry's waste, so the executives penned an open letter to Burberry online. In it they implored the company to reconsider destroying the clothing due to the environmental and anti-humanitarian effects. Instead, thredUp wanted Burberry to allow the secondhand business to sell the leftover products, with the revenue going to an environmental charity of Burberry's choice.

The public response was swift and staggering. As the open letter circulated, consumers clearly agreed with thredUp and joined the business in pressuring the luxury brand to reconsider its policy. By September, Burberry issued a statement on the matter. It agreed that it would no longer burn leftover products and would increase efforts to recycle its clothing. It even went a step further by stating that it would also ban real fur in the manufacturing of its clothing and accessories—a move that likely helped win back some of its most environmentally conscious customers. This case resulted in a positive outcome, but the tactic that accomplished this change was unquestionably online shaming.

and comments and believing that I should no longer work with infants. Thankfully, this never happened."[26]

AIMING TO EMBARRASS

One of the most common objectives of online shaming is to embarrass the victim. People with smartphones photograph or film public interactions they find humorous. Shoppers often snap pictures of fellow customers to mock their appearance or behavior online. Although the photo takers find the situation funny in the moment, they may not consider that the subject is a real person with real feelings. Karma Lawrence acted in this inconsiderate way when she visited a Trader Joe's in New Jersey one day in 2018.

Lawrence recognized one of the grocery store's cashiers as an actor from a popular 1980s sitcom. Geoffrey Owens became famous when he played Elvin on *The Cosby Show*. No longer working steadily as an actor, Owens took the job at Trader Joe's to help support his family. He never viewed the position as beneath him; he simply saw it as a way to earn an honest living. Nevertheless, he was hurt when he learned that Lawrence had taken photos of him when he wasn't looking, and then posted them to social media. Internet users immediately began circulating the images, surprised that a famous person would take such a job.

Lawrence has since said that she regrets sharing the pictures. "I don't know why I snuck a picture," she told *People*. "I actually wanted to go up to him and say something, but I thought, you might embarrass him. But then I did something that actually embarrassed him more. I didn't go with my first instinct, and I should've."[27]

Fortunately, for Owens, this story had a happy ending. As the photos circulated on the internet, numerous people began speaking up for him and his obvious work ethic. They were outraged that he was being shamed for be willing to work a simple job. The story even led to new job offers in the acting field. But most people who end up the victims of online shaming aren't so lucky.

> **"**I actually wanted to go up to him and say something, but I thought, you might embarrass him. But then I did something that actually embarrassed him more. I didn't go with my first instinct, and I should've.**"** 27
>
> *– Karma Lawrence, on when she saw actor Geoffrey Owens working at Trader Joe's*

WHEN THE BULLY FEELS JUSTIFIED

Shaming has become particularly common among people and groups who see their online posts as helpful to society. For example, the internet has become a powerful tool for police departments who post images of people caught dealing drugs or committing sex crimes. People have argued whether this method of punishing the individuals is an ethical move. Jennifer Jacquet, author of *Is Shame Necessary? New Uses for an Old Tool*, thinks it is indeed principled. In her book she wrote, "When shame works without destroying anyone's life, when it leads to reform and reintegration against bad behavior, shaming is performing optimally."28

Problems can occur, though, when an individual rushes to post online without all the facts. In 2015, a woman was shopping at a department store in Australia with her young children. While they were in the toy section, she noticed a man taking pictures of her kids. Alarmed by the apparent behavior of this stranger, the woman snapped a picture of the man taking photos. She then posted the image to her Facebook page, warning others about his behavior.

The post quickly went viral, with thousands of people sharing it to warn others about this person. The problem was that he hadn't taken a photo of the woman's children; he had taken a selfie in front of a Star Wars display for his own kids who were big fans of the movie series.

As the post gained traction on the popular social media platform, one of the man's friends recognized him and shared the post with him. Soon others contacted him as well, some making death threats to him. Knowing that he was completely innocent, the man went straight to the police department, who investigated the matter and cleared him of any wrongdoing. He agreed to speak with the *Daily Mail Australia* on the condition that they not use his name. He told the reporter he was flabbergasted when he learned of the situation. "I'm a father of three kids and a normal human being. . . . I've never taken a selfie before. . . . All of a sudden my name is smeared."[29]

The woman, who also insisted on anonymity in press coverage of the matter, apologized in interviews. She admitted that she should have let the police handle the matter instead of posting about the situation on social media. Regardless of the fact that the man was not guilty of any crimes—or of how sorry the woman felt for her actions—the damage had already been done.

WALTER PALMER

In 2015, Walter Palmer visited the African nation of Zimbabwe to participate in a hunting safari. People often disagree about whether trophy hunting is an acceptable sport, but this particular situation was intensified by Palmer's choice of targets. While in Africa, he used a bow and arrow to shoot and kill Cecil, a thirteen-year-old lion that was revered by people both near and far. Cecil had become a bit of a celebrity in his homeland and had been part of a research

The death of Cecil the Lion caused a massive backlash against Walter Palmer. Online shaming escalated to threats.

project with Oxford University when he was killed by Palmer, a dentist from Minnesota.

Palmer was unaware of Cecil's celebrity status, and he paid $54,000 for the hunt. One of the problems with the killing was that Cecil spent most of his time in the Hwange National Park, which did not allow hunting. Palmer's hunting party lured the animal from this protected area to the nearby Antoinette Farm, which also was not a legal place to hunt lions. Still, Palmer was never charged with any crime. This outraged wildlife enthusiasts, particularly those who were already familiar with Cecil.

When news of the killing broke, people headed to social media to express their disapproval. The story quickly gained momentum. Even celebrities weighed in on the matter. Sharon Osborne, a cohost on the talk show *The Talk*, tweeted, "I don't know how anyone could go to this man for dental services after this. He is a killer. Beware!"[30]

Internet users from all over the world chimed in, with a large majority of the posts shaming Palmer for his actions. Many of these people were saddened by the loss. Many were also upset over the profound impact trophy hunting has on conservation. Some people, however, seemingly joined in just to see Palmer suffer.

Guy Aitchison was an Irish Research Council fellow at University College Dublin. In an interview with the *Telegraph*, he explained that when people feel powerless to make a difference politically, they often head to social media to gain a sense of control, however misguided that effort might be. "It's a relatively low-cost way to feel like you are doing something noble," Atchison said. "But there are also darker motivations at work; the psychic pleasure in seeing someone else brought low and humiliated."[31] Palmer temporarily had to leave his dental practice after he and his family received death threats.

> "It's a relatively low-cost way to feel like you are doing something noble. But there are also darker motivations at work; the psychic pleasure in seeing someone else brought low and humiliated." [31]
>
> – Researcher Guy Aitchison, offering his thoughts on online shaming, 2018

SHAMING AS PUNISHMENT

Using public humiliation to punish children is nothing new. Just a few decades ago, children who acted up in school were forced to stand in a corner of their classroom in front of the rest of the students. Some teachers opted to write a misbehaving child's name on the blackboard instead. Long ago, some teachers made students who were caught chewing gum place the gum on their noses. In all these situations the goal was the same: to embarrass the kids for their actions.

As with other forms of shaming, the internet has added a new layer to this strategy to discourage unwanted behavior in children. In the modern era, some parents post photos or statements about their kids' unwanted behavior online. In 2018, a mother in Ontario, Canada, forced her two sons to walk 4.35 miles (7 km) from their home to their elementary school as a punishment for being rude to their bus driver. To drive the point home even further, she made the boys hold a sign that explained why they were walking to anyone who saw them. Parents who use this type of strategy hope that they are discouraging their children from behaving poorly again, but experts say this public shaming can have a severely negative effect on a child's self-esteem.

CALLING OUT CHEATERS

It is easy to justify public shaming when the target's behavior lies outside what society deems acceptable. This kind of shaming has become so common that observers often see the shaming as a natural consequence. But is shaming a natural effect or the result of a concerted effort? Sue Scheff and Melissa Schorr are the authors of *Shame Nation: Choosing Kindness and Compassion in an Age of Cruelty and Trolling*. In their book they state, "We shame to pressure outliers to conform to our norms—even if no one can agree anymore what those standards should be."[32]

Although it is difficult to gauge how many husbands and wives cheat on their spouses, the percentage of people who think this behavior is morally wrong has increased over the last several decades—from around 65 percent in 1973 to about 81 percent in 2008. Whether the person who cheats is married or in a long-term relationship, cheating often evokes strong feelings of betrayal from the cheater's partner. It can lead to big life changes, such as breakups or divorce. Because so many people see cheating as wrong, it also leads to judgment from people outside the relationship.

This has led to the creation of websites that shame people involved in extramarital affairs. Husbands or wives who discover an extramarital affair can log on to these sites anonymously and post stories about their spouse's infidelities, along with photos of the participants. Some of the sites even allow the posters to include the names and addresses of the individuals. The premise is that people will think twice about starting a relationship with someone who is married if that affair could lead to public shaming.

Although many people think these sites promote hate and cyberbullying, they remain enormously popular based on the number of visitors they receive. One such site, *She's a Homewrecker*, has an accompanying Facebook page with more than 248,000 members. A similar site called *He's a Homewrecker* is also popular. While some might imagine that posting this personal information would be illegal, the law typically works in favor of the posters if what they are posting is true.

Still, not everyone agrees that this public shaming is justifiable. It isn't just the individuals who commit adultery who are hurt by the posts. Their families, including children, can also feel the stigma attached to the virtual flogging the cheaters receive for their actions. In an article about online shaming for *JSTOR Daily*, journalist Farah Mohammed wrote, "It may be what we want in the moment—the satisfaction of having someone who hurt someone else retreat in remorse. But the lasting damaging effects of this, and the fear it spreads, might do more harm than the sense of justice does us good."[33]

"It may be what we want in the moment—the satisfaction of having someone who hurt someone else retreat in remorse. But the lasting damaging effects of this, and the fear it spreads, might do more harm than the sense of justice does us good." [33]

– Farah Mohammed, a journalist writing about online shaming, 2018

CHAPTER THREE

WHAT GROUPS ARE MOST OFTEN TARGETS OF ONLINE SHAMING AND BULLYING?

Certain groups are more likely than others to become the targets of bullies. Girls, for example, find themselves on the receiving end of this type of harassment more often than boys. A 2018 survey of 10,000 students in England found that one in three girls reported being bullied within the previous year, while one in four boys reported being on the receiving end of bullying during that same time frame. The results indicated that girls were also twice as likely to experience cyberbullying.

Girls are actually less likely to become the victims of physical bullying, but the ways girls are harassed are often harder for parents, teachers, and other adults to recognize. A physical altercation often leaves marks on a person's body, but name calling and social exclusion leave no visible evidence. This does not mean that the bullying does not have a lasting effect on the victim, but emotional injuries can be much more difficult for people outside the situation to identify.

To compound the matter, when a victim retaliates authorities can misunderstand the situation. The authorities might only see the

Girls are often bullied in different ways than boys. Exclusion and insults are harder for adults to notice than physical violence.

retaliation and assume the original victim is the aggressor. This can often make it more difficult to resolve the problem. Tom Bennett, an adviser to the Department for Education in England, explained this in an interview with the *Guardian*: "The complexity of who is the bully and who is the bullied also often makes policing this sphere unbelievably difficult, and the inexorable move of such activities online presents huge challenges to even the most concerned teacher."[34]

MELANIA TRUMP'S INITIATIVE AGAINST BULLYING

For more than a century, each first lady of the United States has chosen a cause about which she feels particularly passionate. She then becomes an avid promoter of that cause. Laura Bush shared her love of books and reading with young children, and Michelle Obama promoted childhood health and fitness. When Melania Trump became first lady in 2017, she decided to raise awareness about bullying. Because many of her husband's critics viewed him as a bully, they cried hypocrisy at his wife's choice of causes. But this did not stop Mrs. Trump from doing what she said she felt was right.

Her "Be Best" initiative focuses on healthy living, encouragement, kindness, and respect. It also works to teach kids to use the internet and social media in positive ways. Mrs. Trump said she thinks American culture has become too mean and too rough, especially in the way it treats young people. She wants to bring awareness to the downsides of the internet, which has become a popular setting for kids to bully and mock each other. She hopes that she can help lessen these problems for today's youth by encouraging kids to be their best selves.

Former friends can become bullies too. In an article she wrote for *Psychology Today*, social worker Signe Whitson explained, "One of the things that makes relational bullying so insidious is its under-the-radar nature. It is things left unsaid and invitations not given. It is unexplained cut-offs in friendship. It is silence."[35]

When many people think of cyberbullying, they imagine nasty comments posted publicly to a victim's social media account. However, one of the most powerful tools at a cyberbully's disposal is the unfriend button. Sometimes a bully will encourage or pressure others to take part in a mass unfriending of a bullying victim. The result may not be obvious to anyone but the recipient of this act, but to the victim the message is unmistakable and overwhelming.

Although bullies often prey on perceived weaknesses, many times the victim of bullying may have many strong and envied qualities. Girls who are considered pretty, smart, or likeable by their peers can often become the targets of bullies who feel threatened by these traits. In a situation like this, the bully begins to harass her target in an effort to make her feel less confident. The bully might see herself as leveling the playing field, but what she might not realize is how much she is hurting the victim.

WOMEN AS TARGETS AND PERPETRATORS

People often remark about how cruel kids can be, but some experts point to adult female role models as examples young female bullies imitate. Experts look at women role models because bullying is a common problem between young girls. Dr. Gail Cross, who specializes in human behavior, parenting, and education, wrote in a piece for the *Huffington Post*, "When women bully, and they do, it is often related to both competition and judgment. Judgment offers control and it has the capacity to lead to cruelty."[36] If a mother bullies other women in her life, this negative behavior can set a powerful example for her daughter.

When women aren't the targets of other women, they often face bullying from men. In many instances this harassment happens online. Although men can certainly be victims of bullying, the reasons they are bullied differ drastically from why women are victimized. A *Time* article by Soraya Chemaly about online harassment points out,

> "The harassment targeted at men is not *because they are men*, as is clearly more frequently the case with women. It's defining because a lot of harassment is an effort to put women, because they are women, back in their 'place.'"[37]
>
> – Soraya Chemaly, writer

"The harassment targeted at men is not *because they are men*, as is clearly more frequently the case with women. It's defining because a lot of harassment is an effort to put women, because they are women, back in their 'place.'"[37]

Men who bully often take extreme measures in trying to intimidate their female victims. They use dominance to frighten, punish, or silence the women they target. And the internet becomes an effective tool for accomplishing these goals.

Many times, a man's online bullying victim is an ex-wife or former girlfriend. When a relationship ends, particularly one that was abusive in some way, a man might turn to the internet as a last-ditch effort to change his significant other's mind about the breakup or as a means of exacting revenge. According to the National Domestic Violence Hotline, men who bully their exes online often post unwanted messages or photos to the women's social media pages, hack into their email accounts, or even create fake online profiles to trick the women into thinking that they are communicating with someone else.

Women may even be targeted online by men they have only recently met or don't know at all. The nature of the bullying in these cases is often sexual. A 2017 survey of women between the ages of eighteen and twenty-nine years old revealed that 21 percent had been sexually harassed online. This is more than double the percentage of men from the same age group who reported online harassment.

42

The end of a romantic relationship can lead to bullying. Former partners may bully in an effort to get back together or to seek revenge.

Fifty-three percent of the women between these ages also reported that they had received explicit images that they did not request.

One of the things that makes the battle to stop the online bullying of women so difficult is the disparity between men's and women's attitudes about it. According to the Pew Research Center, 43 percent of men said that online spaces should be welcoming and safe for visitors, while 63 percent of women believe this. In keeping with this thinking, a higher percentage of men believe it is more important for people to speak their minds freely online than to keep online spaces free from bullying. While 83 percent of young women say that online harassment is a major problem, only 55 percent of young men agree. When so many people do not view an issue as problematic, it is difficult to find a solution.

TARGETED FOR SPEAKING UP

Speaking up about a matter that upsets other people can lead those people to target the whistleblower. In grade school, telling a teacher that another student has broken the rules might lead that student's friends to pick on the so-called tattletale. Even the teacher may tell the student to stop tattling. Sadly, this kind of bullying doesn't stop in adulthood, and the stakes can be tremendous.

During the summer of 2018, President Donald Trump nominated Brett Kavanaugh to the US Supreme Court. As with any nominee, the Senate needed to confirm Kavanaugh before he could take the open seat on the highest court in the United States. Before the full Senate votes to confirm a new Supreme Court justice, the Senate Judiciary Committee reviews the nominee. Hearings take place in which witnesses testify to the character and past actions of the nominee. Shortly after Trump selected Kavanaugh, a woman from the nominee's past wrote a letter to a member of the committee. Through this correspondence, Christine Blasey Ford told Senator Dianne Feinstein that Brett Kavanaugh had sexually assaulted her years earlier when they were both high school students in Maryland. Still, Ford was hesitant to appear in front of the Senate. The letter, which was later released to the media, prompted intense reactions from the media and the public leading up to Ford's testimony in front of the Senate in September. Kavanaugh, however, vehemently denied that this assault had taken place.

Dr. Christine Blasey Ford and her family received death threats after she publicly accused a Supreme Court nominee of sexual assault. This treatment is common in controversial political testimonies.

As Ford read her opening statement to the Senate on September 27, 2018, she described more recent experiences about how she and her family had been treated since her name was released to the public. She said,

My family and I have been the target of constant harassment and death threats. I have been called the most vile and hateful names imaginable. These messages, while far fewer than the expressions of support, have been terrifying to receive and have rocked me to my core. People have posted my personal information on the internet. This has resulted in additional emails, calls, and threats. My family and I were forced to move out of our home. Since September 16, my family and I have been living in various secure locales, with guards. This past Tuesday evening, my work email account was hacked and messages were sent out supposedly recanting my description of the sexual assault.[38]

Politics can bring out rude behavior in many people. Republicans and Democrats alike often feel passionate about their political beliefs, leading them into heated discussions with people whose minds they hope to change. When the people in these discussions do not remain respectful of each other, though, mayhem can ensue. Many of these discussions take place in online forums, leading some participants to bully one another. In the situation of Christine Blasey Ford, however, many people—including journalists—overlooked the fact that Ford's reputation and safety were being put at risk. Many people used the internet as a soapbox from which to shame her, while some people even tried to bully her out of testifying.

While the media did not make the threats to Ford, journalists were determined to share her story from a variety of perspectives. Some of the stories framed her as a victim of sexual assault; others characterized her as liar with her own political agenda. The same day that Ford testified, Alexandria Neason and Nausicaa Renner wrote an article for the *Columbia Journalism Review* in which they stated,

"We are taught to push past the inevitable discomfort, to ignore the triggering of our internal barometers of empathy, and then to wear that feat as badge of honor. This, we are told, is part of what makes journalism not merely a job but a calling."[39]

BULLIES TARGETING RACIAL MINORITIES AND WOMEN

In 2018, an Oregon news station ran a story about a biracial student being bullied in the city of Lake Oswego. The thirteen-year-old boy wasn't named in the piece, but his mother, Jennifer Cook, shared his story, as well as her own heartbreak over the situation. As her son sat in school, classmates had handed him a note containing a racial slur, clearly directed at him. When the boy told his mother about the incident, she began asking him questions, which led to an alarming response from the child. He told his mother that he was used to being treated this way, and that he often heard the slur as many as twenty times a day at his school.

The same news story also detailed students recently finding racist graffiti in the bathroom at Lake Oswego High School. This situation prompted a group of students to stage a walkout during school hours to show their support for the teens who were being targeted due to their race. The school district provided a quote for the news story, stating that it did not tolerate hate speech, bullying, or harassment, but that problems like these are not easily solved. Some parents in the district

> "You shouldn't need diversity to be able to know how to treat other human beings."[40]
>
> – Mia Smith, friend of a family with a bullied son

responded by saying that the problem was unlikely to be solved until the district included more people from racial minority groups. Mia Smith, a friend of Jennifer Cook, disagreed. She told the news station, "You shouldn't need diversity to be able to know how to treat other human beings."[40]

According to a study by Georgia State University, women and people of color—both male and female—face higher rates of bullying in the workplace. It isn't just the victim's fellow employees who may be guilty of this kind of bullying. Often, it is a person's superior who uses racial slurs, makes inappropriate jokes about gender or race, or gives the least desirable tasks to women or people of color. These are just a few of the ways that workplace bullying might be carried out, but the problem is definitely not limited to these behaviors. Many times the treatment may be more subtle, such as ignoring employees of color or not taking their contributions seriously. These less overt forms of bullying are still harmful to the people on the receiving end of the treatment, especially when the negative treatment is ongoing. When bullying is motivated by differences such as race or gender, it can be a form of racism or sexism.

One thing that makes the workplace bullying of women and people of color so difficult to stop is that many employees who witness the mistreatment do not speak up. Women and black employees in particular report that they do not have social support at work that could help prevent the bullying. What's more, both groups reported feeling heavily affected by the harassment, which can lead to poor work performance. Brandon K. Attell, the lead researcher for a Georgia State University study, explained that dealing with this problem instead of continuing to ignore it could make the workplace a more pleasant and productive environment for everyone. "If workplace bullying can be prevented, individuals will experience less stress at work and will in turn have better mental health. Additionally, employees who are less stressed are more loyal to their organizations, perform better on the job, and have less absenteeism."[41]

THE LGBT COMMUNITY

Another group that experiences high rates of bullying is LGBT youth. Young LGBT people are subjected to online harassment three times more often than straight kids. In fact, a national survey of kids between the ages of twelve and seventeen revealed that the most likely group of kids to be bullied are those who are LGBT or simply perceived to be LGBT.

"If workplace bullying can be prevented, individuals will experience less stress at work and will in turn have better mental health. Additionally, employees who are less stressed are more loyal to their organizations, perform better on the job, and have less absenteeism."[41]

– Brandon K. Attell, lead researcher for a Georgia State University study about bullying

In many school districts, kids are encouraged to seek out a teacher or other authority figure if they are being bullied. However, adults do not always provide safe spaces for LGBT youth. Almost 64 percent of kids who identify as lesbian, gay, bisexual, or transgender report that they have heard homophobic remarks from school staff members. It is difficult for students to ask for help from adults who are perpetuating the problem.

Parents of LGBT students may or may not be helpful in these situations, depending on the level of support they give their kids at home. Dr. Mark Schuster led a study on bullying that was published in the *New England Journal of Medicine*. He thinks it is important for parents not to make fun of LGBT people. In some cases they may be making their own children feel rejected. "For the kids who aren't sexual minorities," he added, "it's also sending a message that it's okay to mock people who are gay."[42]

Like people from other minority groups, people who identify as LGBT continue to be targeted as adults in the workplace. More than half of these workers say that repeated bullying is a problem for them at work. Michael Erwin, who heads communications and social media at CareerBuilder, has said that employers need to take action in these incidents: "Bullying of any kind or of anyone has no place in the workplace—period. Employers have a responsibility to create a safe working environment for all employees. They can minimize this destructive behavior by offering sensitivity training and enforcing anti-bullying policies across their organizations."[43]

PEOPLE WITH DISABILITIES

Kids with disabilities face the highest risk of being bullied. In fact, numerous studies have found that a child with a disability is three times more likely to be bullied than nondisabled peers. To make matters worse for the victims, kids with severe developmental disabilities might also be less able to report incidents of harassment.

The StopBullying.gov website offers some insight into what can help most in solving this problem. The site states, "One reason children and young adults with special health care needs might be at higher risk for bullying is a lack of peer support. Having friends who are respected by peers can prevent and protect against bullying."[44] The site also discusses strategies some schools have implemented to help combat this type of bullying. One school, for example, organized a wheelchair soccer night during which students who use wheelchairs

People with disabilities frequently face bullying. It often occurs on public transportation.

acted as coaches by teaching their peers how to use them to play the game. Another school formed a weekly lunch program for kids during which kids with disabilities were paired with nondisabled children to spend their lunchtime together, getting to know one another. Programs like this one can lay the foundation for friendships that can help decrease bullying.

BULLYING AND WEIGHT

Kids are often bullied because of their weight. In many cases, the child who becomes the target is overweight, but underweight children are also at an increased risk of being bullied. While girls are most commonly targeted, boys are bullied due to their body size too. Some 30 percent of middle school girls and 24 percent of boys the same age report experiencing bullying due to their weight. And the effects can be destructive, leading to problems such as depression, anxiety, and eating disorders.

It is easy to picture a typical bully in a situation like this—a mean yet popular girl at school who falls within her own ideal weight range—but the guilty party isn't always who one might expect. Sometimes the bully is a sibling or even an adult such as an athletic coach or a parent. Sometimes these bullies do not even realize they are in fact bullying, but a lack of intention does not excuse the behavior.

As with so many other types of harassment, the internet has extended this kind of bullying. Pictures posted online with hateful comments can circulate quickly, pressuring the victim to go to extremes to change their body size. At the Meadows Ranch, a treatment center for anorexia in Wickenburg, Arizona, almost 50 percent of the adolescent and young adult patients reported having been bullied about their body size.

With a majority of impairments acquired after people reach adulthood, though, bullying is a problem many disabled people face regardless of age. Penny Pepper is a writer and disability rights activist in the United Kingdom. She is also a disabled adult who has said that she deals with bullying on what seems to be a weekly basis. She thinks that part of the problem is that nondisabled people often exclude people with disabilities from society. "Exclusion," she wrote in a 2017 article for the *Guardian*, "has defined disabled people in the public imagination as being powerless, and lacking fundamental rights. And this stigmatization and alienation, in my experience, drives an increase in bullying and abuse."[45] Pepper notes that people with disabilities can lose their freedom to travel if they lack assistance in doing things as simple as getting out of bed or arranging transportation. And if they can't travel, it becomes harder to socialize and get involved in their community. Pepper says, "Frankly, non-disabled society forgets you exist and when you fight to break out of this exclusion, to claim your rightful place in society, you suddenly become an easy target."[46]

CHAPTER FOUR

HOW CAN SOCIETY PREVENT ONLINE SHAMING AND BULLYING?

Because online shaming and bullying are difficult to prevent, it can be easy to feel discouraged about them. Some people even dismiss the problem as one that cannot be fully solved. Many experts point out that while society is working on correcting the problem, there is obviously still much left to be done. Author Kristen Houghton wrote an article for the *Huffington Post* called "Why We Can't Stop Bullying." In the piece she points out, "In the past few years, schools have begun themes and discussions on stopping the harassment of children by other children. They role-play bullying in school assemblies, teach tactics for defusing situations, and stress respect for everyone. Educators say that it is working, but is it really? There are too many instances that say it is not."[47]

Numerous experts think that this is a case where prevention can be the most effective solution. Anti-bullying programs help raise awareness about the issue, which is a start, but follow-through is also an essential component in stopping the problem. Teachers and other authority figures cannot simply stage assemblies and hang posters about bullying. Adults need to remain watchful of student behavior.

Teachers, parents, and authorities try to stop bullying. Despite their efforts, bullying still happens.

Moreover, when accusations are made, they must be taken seriously, or kids will be less likely to report instances of bullying in the future, making real change difficult.

A lot of bullying begins in schools, but social media platforms are where it morphs into a problem much more challenging to manage. In 2016, the Duke and Duchess of Cambridge (Prince William and his wife, Catherine), took steps to combat this problem by creating the Royal Foundation Taskforce on the Prevention of Cyberbullying. While visiting a school west of London, the couple spoke with students about the importance of not spending too much time on the internet. Prince William told the students, "Don't spend all day online. Seriously,

> "Don't spend all day online. Seriously, don't. For your mental health, get outside, come away from the screen. By all means be on a screen, but don't be on it all day because it will only bring you into another world. It's important that you balance the time."[48]
>
> – England's Prince William, the Duke of Cambridge

don't. For your mental health, get outside, come away from the screen." He acknowledged that the internet has its usefulness. "By all means be on a screen," he said, "but don't be on it all day because it will only bring you into another world. It's important that you balance the time."[48]

Many other famous people have also joined the anti-bullying cause, hoping to make a difference. More than one hundred celebrities—including comedian and talk show host Ellen DeGeneres, journalist Hoda Kotb, and musician Charlie Puth—work with Stomp Out Bullying, a national organization that works to stop all kinds of bullying for kids and teens in the United States. Some of the celebrities who lend their names and images to this cause experienced bullying firsthand before they became famous. For example, recording artist Demi Lovato has said that she was severely bullied in school for her weight.

WHAT SOCIAL MEDIA MOGULS ARE DOING

With so much bullying taking place online, many people look to social media platforms as the biggest influences in stopping online shaming and harassment. A 2018 survey in the United Kingdom found that 83 percent of people want social media companies to do more to stop cyberbullying. Despite all the good things that social media

ANTI-BULLYING LEGISLATION AND POLICIES

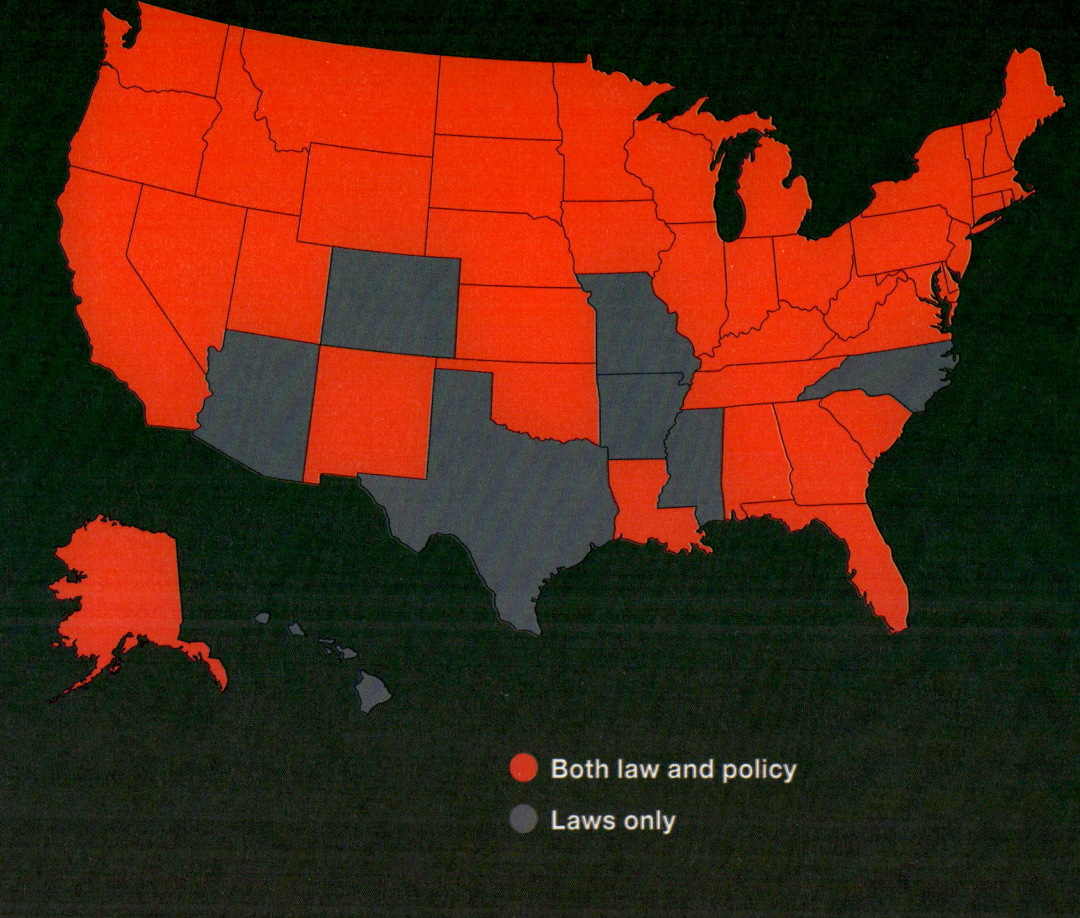

- Both law and policy
- Laws only

All fifty states have passed anti-bullying laws. Not every state has additional policies regarding bullying too. Laws and policies can have different effects and include different language. Some define what is considered bullying, include protected groups such as people of color, outline sentencing for someone convicted of bullying, and much more. Still, with these laws and policies in place, the problem has not stopped.

"Laws, Policies & Regulations," StopBullying.gov, n.d. www.stopbullying.gov.

has brought to the world, these services have become a significant platform for bullying, so many anti-bullying advocates think these companies bear a responsibility to stop it.

Facebook CEO Mark Zuckerberg recognized his responsibility to make his social media service a better place in January 2018. He announced that this goal would be his New Year's resolution. "The world feels anxious and divided, and Facebook has a lot of work to do—whether it's protecting our community from abuse and hate, defending against interference by nation states, or making sure that time spent on Facebook is time well spent. My personal challenge for 2018 is to focus on fixing these important issues."[49]

In October 2018, the company announced more tangible measures to back up Zuckerberg's promise. Facebook unveiled new tools for eliminating bullying behavior on both its website and certain cell phone apps. One of these measures included a way for users to report bullying on a friend's behalf when they witness this behavior. After a complaint is received, a team working for the company will investigate it to determine whether it violates Facebook's rules. The new changes also gave users the ability to delete or hide entire groups of comments instead of having to remove them one at a time. They also allowed users to block offensive words.

Some people criticized Facebook for the amount of time it took the company to create and enact these changes. They drew attention to the fact that Instagram had been helping its users block offensive words for years. Around the same time that Facebook was rolling out its changes in 2018, Instagram announced it had added technology that detects bullying in photos as well. As the tech identifies potentially problematic images, it sends them to a human team to review them before removal. After announcing these anti-bullying measures,

Facebook has taken steps to help stop cyberbullying. Reporting a problematic post for a friend can help stop the problem.

Adam Mosseri, the new head of the company, also admitted that Instagram's work against the problem was far from over. "Online bullying is complex," he said, "and we know we have more work to do to further limit bullying and spread kindness on Instagram."[50]

TURNING HATE INTO ART AND AWARENESS

A few people have set amazing examples of how to turn online shaming into something positive. In 2014, Lindsay Bottos, a twenty-one-year-old art student at the Maryland Institute College of Art, was sharing her art on the internet. Although she received positive feedback from her intended audience, she also found that she was attracting unwanted attention from internet trolls. These online bullies look for ways to attack and hurt others with their words, as if doing so is a game.

Bottos often posted pictures of herself along with photos of her art to Tumblr; it was these selfies that attracted most of the hateful comments. Users quickly began sending her anonymous messages, critiquing her appearance as if she were an object rather than a person. People focused heavily on what they saw as her flaws, commenting on her acne, her tattoos, and even the amount of hair they saw growing under her arms in the photos. They also sexually harassed her. Bottos said, "I get tons of anonymous messages like this every day and while this isn't unique to women, the content of the messages and the frequency in which I get them are definitely related to my gender."[51] In addition to calling her ugly, the posters used offensive language to accuse her of being promiscuous. One even expressed a wish that she would die from a sexually transmitted disease.

Most people would be taken aback by comments like these, and Bottos was no exception, but she refused to be defined as a victim in this situation. She decided to take the comments and use them in her art. She transformed them into captions for a new series of photos of herself, each with a different pose and facial expression. Titled Anonymous, the series called attention to the disturbing problem of cyberbullying. The trolls had tried to hurt her, but she transformed their words into something positive. She in turn became an activist as well as an artist.

Bottos thinks that people are more likely to make nasty or threatening comments online because they can hide behind a username. She explained to the *Baltimore Sun*, "The anonymity allows people to say whatever they want without any consequences.

Cyberbullies can hide behind usernames when they post hurtful comments. These people are often called internet trolls.

They want to get a reaction, to bring you down."[52] In her case, however, they ended up giving both her and the important topic of bullying a great deal of positive attention. Her series received tens of thousands of responses on Tumblr.

MINIMIZING THE RISKS OF BEING CYBERBULLIED

Putting an end to all bullying is an obvious long-term goal, but with the problem so widespread, teens need practical and specific strategies they can use every day to protect themselves from

61

becoming targets. Bullying victims are not responsible for the behavior of their tormentors, but educating kids can help them recognize a potentially harmful situation before it becomes a problem. Bullying is almost always carried out with an audience, so it is important to teach kids to seek help if they notice that a peer is being bullied. Not all teasing or joking—online or otherwise—is bullying, but if a child feels uncomfortable, it is time to discuss the situation with an adult.

Some parents may think the best defense against online shaming and bullying is blocking kids from social media, but many experts warn against this approach. Social worker Signe Whitson wrote in a 2017 *Psychology Today* article, "At best, this head-in-the-sand approach ill-prepares kids to deal with the world in which they live and at worst, it creates a fervor among these young people to get their hands on social media in sneaky, risky ways."[53]

While it should not be a teen's only form of socialization, many kids between fourteen and seventeen years old view social media as an integral setting for their friendships. In many cases, the connections they feel from being able to bond with peers on these platforms actually add to their social well-being. Problems arise when kids start focusing too much on the virtual world.

A 2018 study of teenagers in Germany, Poland, and Romania revealed that teens who spend more than two hours a day on social media face an increased

> "At best, this head-in-the-sand approach ill-prepares kids to deal with the world in which they live and at worst, it creates a fervor among these young people to get their hands on social media in sneaky, risky ways."[53]
>
> – Signe Whitson, social worker

risk of cyberbullying. This research project, which surveyed more than 12,000 teens, indicated that moderation could be a key step in keeping young people safer on social media apps and sites. Monitoring is also important. By keeping computers and devices in common areas of the home, parents can watch teens to make sure that their interactions are safe. Parents should also make sure that kids meet the minimum age requirement before joining any site. Younger kids are often less able to recognize high-risk behaviors, such as sharing too much personal information online.

Another thing that parents should watch for is a preoccupation with social status. Dr. Jonathan B. Singer is an assistant professor of social work at Temple University. He pointed out that a focus on social status can be possible a red flag with bullying. "Victims and perpetrators of cyberbullying tend to have issues with self-esteem, anger, frustration, poor social skills, or obsession with social status." He adds that having one or more of these problems does not necessarily mean a child is bullying or being bullied, "but it is a warning sign, and something that parents should look out for."[54]

BULLIES HAVE PARENTS TOO

Many parents worry about their kids becoming the victims of bullies, but they should also be concerned about their children becoming bullies themselves. There are relatively few statistics and studies on bullying and the number of kids who take part in it. This makes it especially important that parents remain vigilant. While the data from most studies focuses on the victims, where there is a victim, there is also a perpetrator.

Just as many bullying victims do not always tell their parents what is going on, most bullies do not want to discuss the situation with

It may be challenging for parents to find out that their child is a bully. The child may refuse to discuss the subject openly.

their parents. Nicola Jenkins found this out the hard way when she discovered that her twelve-year-old daughter was posting unkind remarks about her peers online. In an interview with *BBC News*, Jenkins said, "Her friend's mum spoke to me about it and showed me the messages that had been sent. When I approached my daughter about it, she denied that there had been anything going on. It took a while to get it out of her."[55]

Jenkins dealt with the problem by removing her daughter's access to social media for a while, and she spoke to her daughter at length about what is and is not acceptable to post online. When she finally allowed her daughter access to the internet again, she monitored her interactions closely.

Although society has painted a picture of bullies as monsters, parents need to understand that all children are capable of acting as bullies. If a child does bully, the parent has two main responsibilities—first, making sure the child understands that the behavior is unacceptable and second, helping the child develop more empathy for others. Many times kids are so focused on their own goal of achieving or maintaining a high social status that they don't think to look at the situation from the perspective of the victim. Doing so can make a big difference in future behavior.

Another thing that can be helpful is determining the reason for the bullying. In many instances, the bully is going through a rough time and acting out because of it. During an episode of the NPR program *Talk of the Nation*, host Neal Conan took a call from a woman named Brenda who admitted that she had been a bully in junior high school. One day during the eighth grade, Brenda began picking on a girl from her Brownie troop out of the blue. She said that at the time she didn't realize why she was doing it, but the reason became clear when she reflected on the experience as an adult: Brenda was being bullied herself by another girl. "She harassed me horribly," Brenda said. "I was miserable. And what occurs to me now is nobody ever asked me. You know, when I went to the principal's office, they didn't ask me, you know, is somebody doing this to you?"[56]

STOPPING BULLYING ONCE IT HAS BEGUN

Among the most effective strategies that can help put an end to bullying is building a strong social network. A victim may never become friends with his or her bully, but having a wide circle of friends

MEDIA CAN HELP

Just as social media has provided an easy setting for online bullying, the media in general can help solve the problem by bringing attention to it. News agencies—in print, on television, or online—can use their massive reach to raise awareness of how prevalent bullying has become. Human interest stories about the issue can show active or potential bullies the harm that they can cause through this harassment. These news pieces can also show victims that they are not alone.

Although many people blame social media for contributing to bullying, many apps and sites have become places where bullying victims can seek support, finding a community of people who understand what they are going through. In this way, social media can be a source of solutions as well. Social media sites continue to add tools for people who feel targeted. For example, Facebook has created a feature for one user to request that the service remove a different user's content. Likewise, Instagram allows users to completely disable the comment feature on their photos. And Snapchat notifies users if someone screenshots one of their snaps.

makes bullying victims feel less alone. Isolation is one of the ways that bullies maintain control of others. Additionally, having a group of supportive friends makes a person less vulnerable to being targeted. People who need to build a social network can meet new friends through joining clubs based on their hobbies, trying out for sports teams, or connecting with people at work. The old saying that there is strength in numbers is often true.

Friends and other bystanders can help stop bullying first and foremost by not taking part in it. The worst thing an observer can do is join the bully in harassing the victim, but more passive behaviors such as laughing, sharing embarrassing online posts, or even just watching can perpetuate the mistreatment. The National Education Association's website states, "Bystanders provide bullies an audience, and often actually encourage bullying."[57]

Sometimes speaking up for the victim and calling the behavior what it is can help. Tell the perpetrator that the behavior is bullying and to stop it. One doesn't even have to know the victim to help stop the bullying. Anyone can report the behavior to a person in a position of authority. In an online setting, report the behavior to administrators. Doing so may or may not stop the bullying, but it is a smart place to start.

Unfortunately, taking the matter to a person in charge sometimes falls far short of solving the problem. In the worst cases, it can even exacerbate the problem. The accused bully might become defensive or begin making greater efforts in turning others against the alleged victim. Bullies may also retaliate against the victim for getting them in trouble. When a child is accused of bullying, sometimes the parents take a defensive stance. When school officials step in after bullying has been reported, the bullying often gets worse. Either the bully or victim often wind up resenting the school for stepping into the situation. The bully might resent the school and attack the victim more, or the victim might resent the school for making the situation worse.

Although bullying is a complicated matter, one thing is clear: When schools take sides, the problem almost always worsens. Many experts assert that the best approach is teaching kids the skills they need to deal with this problem. This does not mean leaving them without resources, but rather means providing them with the

Teaching students to talk through their problems can lead to positive solutions. Openness and transparency is one way to respond to bullying and bring it to an end.

resources to solve the problem. Izzy Kalman is the author of *Bullies to Buddies: How to Turn Your Enemies into Friends*. He stresses, "Kids deserve to be taught how to handle such actions on their own. They also deserve to be taught how to defuse physical threats and confrontations, because there isn't always going to be an adult around to save them. Their peers will like and respect them much more if they deal with them directly than if they tell on them. And they will have more self-respect as well."[58]

Online shaming and bullying will not be solved quickly or easily. They will not become less common unless people make a strong effort to better understand these incredibly complicated issues. If anything, bullying is bound to become more complex as technology evolves. By increasing awareness about this problem, society can continue to take positive actions against bullying and the harms it causes.

"Kids deserve to be taught how to handle such actions on their own. They also deserve to be taught how to defuse physical threats and confrontations, because there isn't always going to be an adult around to save them. Their peers will like and respect them much more if they deal with them directly than if they tell on them. And they will have more self-respect as well." [57]

– *Izzy Kalman, author of Bullies to Buddies: How to Turn Your Enemies into Friends*

SOURCE NOTES

INTRODUCTION: BULLYING AND SHAMING TODAY

1. Quoted in Phil Helsel and Joe Fryer, "Denver Mom Whose 9-year-old Killed Himself Pleads for End to Bullying," *NBC News*, August 28, 2018. www.nbcnews.com.

2. Quoted in Helsel and Fryer, "Denver Mom Whose 9-Year-Old Killed Himself Pleads for End to Bullying."

3. Quoted in "The Alarming Increase of Bullying Incidents in Europe Calls for a Common European Strategy," *European Anti-Bullying Network*, December 9, 2015. www.antibullying.eu.

4. Maria Konnikova, "How the Internet Has Changed Bullying," *New Yorker*, October 21, 2015. www.newyorker.com.

5. "6 Ways Educators Can Prevent Bullying in Schools," *Lesley University*, n.d. https://lesley.edu.

6. MaryAnn Byrne, "Bullying Will Never End," *Bullying Education*, n.d. www.bullyingeducation.org.

CHAPTER 1: HOW DID ONLINE SHAMING AND BULLYING BEGIN?

7. Monica Anderson, "A Majority of Teens Have Experienced Some Form of Cyberbullying," *Pew Research Center*, September 27, 2018. www.pewinternet.org.

8. Quoted in "Interview with Scott Poland on the Effects of Bullying and Cyberbullying," *Online MSW Programs*, 2019. www.onlinemswprograms.com.

9. Quoted in "Megan's Story," *Megan Meier Foundation*, n.d. https://meganmeierfoundation.org.

10. Quoted in Tom McCarthy and Scott Michels, "Lori Drew MySpace Suicide Hoax Conviction Thrown Out," *ABC News*, July 2, 2009. abcnews.go.com.

11. Quoted in Mike Celizic, "Her Teen Committed Suicide over 'Sexting,'" *Today*, October 14, 2016. www.today.com.

12. Quoted in Lydia Warren, "Family of Girl, 18, Who Committed Suicide After Boyfriend Texted Naked Photos of Her to Fellow Students Receives $154k from School that 'Failed to Stop Bullying,'" *Daily Mail*, October 9, 2012. www.dailymail.co.uk.

13. Quoted in Randi Kaye, "How a Cell Phone Photo Led to a Girl's Suicide," *CNN*, October 7, 2010. www.cnn.com.

14. Quoted in Caitlin Johnston, "Riverview Mother Strives to Save Children from Suicide," *Tampa Bay Times*, September 19, 2013. www.tampabay.com.

15. Saima Majeed, "Psychological Predictors of Cyber Bullying in Early Adulthood," *Health Science Journal*, February 29, 2016. www.hsj.gr.

16. Quoted in Cindy Long, "Bullying Takes Toll on Minority Student Achievement," *NEA Today*, September 7, 2011. http://neatoday.org.

17. "Official Statement from the Clementi Family Regarding New Jersey State Appeals Court Decision," *Tyler Clementi Foundation*, September 9, 2016. https://tylerclementi.org.

18. Quoted in Jennifer Pike Bailey. "Tyler Clementi Higher Education Anti-Harassment Act Reintroduced in Congress," *Human Rights Campaign*, April 27, 2017. www.hrc.org.

19. Dave Cullen, "Mean Kids 'The Bully Society,' by Jessie Klein," *New York Times,* April 27, 2012. www.nytimes.com.

20. Quoted in Taylor Swaak, "How We Talk About Bullying After School Shootings Can Be Dangerous: Experts," *Newsweek*, February 25, 2018. www.newsweek.com.

21. Anya Kamenetz, "Here's How to Prevent the Next School Shooting, Experts Say," *NPR*, March 7, 2018. www.npr.org.

CHAPTER 2: HOW CAN PEOPLE RECOGNIZE ONLINE SHAMING AND BULLYING?

22. Quoted in Dave Quinn, "Olympic Gymnasts Gabby Douglas and Simone Biles Talk Body Shaming—and How to Beat It," *People*, July 1, 2016. https://people.com.

23. Quoted in Lisa Respers France, "Ariel Winter Is on a Body Shaming Clap Back Mission," *CNN*, May 5, 2017. www.cnn.com.

24. Quoted in *Today with Kathie Lee and Hoda*, December 7, 2018. www.today.com.

25. Quoted in Abby Gardner, "Gabrielle Union Has No Time for People Shaming Her for Kissing Her Baby on the Lips," *Glamour*, December 7, 2018. www.glamour.com.

26. Quoted in Terri Peters, "Here's the Real Story Behind the Viral Photo That Had So Many Judging This Mom," *Today*, December 7, 2018. www.today.com.

27. Quoted in Aurelie Corinthios, "Woman Who Took Geoffrey Owens' Photo at Trader Joe's Says She Didn't Mean to Shame Him," *People*, September 5, 2018. https://people.com.

28. Jennifer Jacquet, *Is Shaming Necessary? New Uses for an Old Tool.* New York: Pantheon, 2015, pp. 168–169.

29. Quoted in Ashley Welch, "Woman Apologizes for Mistakenly Shaming Man on Facebook," *CBS News*, May 11, 2015. www.cbsnews.com.

30. Quoted in Joseph Neese, "How 25 Celebrities Reacted to Cecil the Lion's Death," *MSNBC*, July 31, 2015. www.msnbc.com.

31. Quoted in Mark Molloy, "Online Shaming: The Dangerous Rise of the Internet Pitchfork Mob," *Telegraph*, June 25, 2018. www.telegraph.co.uk.

SOURCE NOTES CONTINUED

32. Sue Scheff and Melissa Schorr, *Shame Nation: Choosing Kindness and Compassion in an Age of Cruelty and Trolling.* Naperville, IL: Sourcebooks, 2017, p. 9.

33. Farah Mohammed, "The Danger of Public Shaming in the Internet Age," *JSTOR Daily*, January 25, 2018. https://daily.jstor.org.

CHAPTER 3: WHAT GROUPS ARE MOST OFTEN TARGETS OF ONLINE SHAMING AND BULLYING?

34. Quoted in Richard Adams, "Girls More Likely to Be Bullied Than Boys, English School Survey Finds," *Guardian*, June 13, 2018. www.theguardian.com.

35. Signe Whitson, "Helping Girls Cope with Bullying and Frenemies," *Psychology Today*, January 12, 2015. www.psychologytoday.com.

36. Gail Cross, "Girls Who Bully and the Women They Learn From," *Huffington Post*, October 3, 2013. www.huffpost.com.

37. Soraya Chemaly, "There's No Comparing Male and Female Harassment Online," *Time*, September 9, 2014. http://time.com.

38. "Christine Blasey Ford's Prepared Testimony," *CNN*, September 27, 2018. www.cnn.com.

39. Alexandria Neason and Nausicaa Renner, "The Media Bullying of Christine Blasey Ford," *Columbia Journalism Review*, September 27, 2018. www.cjr.org.

40. Quoted in Marja Martinez, "Lake Oswego Parent Describes Racial Bullying of Son: 'He Said He Was Upset, but That He's Used to It,'" *Fox 12*, January 30, 2018. www.kptv.com.

41. Quoted in Lori Solomon, "Women, Minorities More Likely To Report Bullying in the Workplace, Georgia State Study Shows," *Georgia State University*, April 4, 2017. https://news.gsu.edu.

42. Quoted in Andrew M. Seamen, "Why LGBT Adolescents Are Still More Likely to Face Bullying, Including Social Exclusion and Physical Harm," *Huffington Post*, May 7, 2016. www.huffpost.com.

43. Quoted in Sue Scheff, "How Workplace Bullying Is Impacting LGBT Employees," *Psychology Today*, October 19, 2017. www.psychologytoday.com.

44. "Bullying and Youth with Disabilities and Special Health Needs," *Stop Bullying*, n.d. www.stopbullying.gov.

45. Penny Pepper, "Bullying of Disabled People Has Got Worse—Because It's Government-Sanctioned," *Guardian*, April 13, 2017. www.theguardian.com.

46. Pepper, "Bullying of Disabled People Has Got Worse—Because It's Government-Sanctioned."

CHAPTER 4: HOW CAN SOCIETY PREVENT ONLINE SHAMING AND BULLYING?

47. Kristen Houghton, "Why We Can't Stop Bullying," *Huffington Post*, November 23, 2013. www.huffpost.com.

48. Quoted in Stephanie Petit, "Kate Middleton and Prince William Are Back to Work After Prince Charles' Birthday Bash," *People*, November 15, 2018. https://people.com.

49. Quoted in Lindsey Bever, "Mark Zuckerberg Pledges 'To Do the Job He Already Has,' Basically," *Washington Post*, January 4, 2018. www.washingtonpost.com.

50. Quoted in Kaya Yurieff, "Instagram Says It Will Now Detect Bullying in Photos," *CNN*, October 9, 2018. www.cnn.com.

51. Quoted in Julianne Ross, "This Young Artist Turns Online Bullying Towards Women into Empowering Art," *Mic*, January 29, 2014. https://mic.com.

52. Quoted in Julie Scharper, "MICA Student Turns Cyber-Bullying into Art," *Baltimore Sun*, January 31, 2014. www.baltimoresun.com.

53. Signe Whitson, "Why Banning Social Media Is Not the Best Answer for Kids," *Psychology Today*, April 7, 2017. www.psychologytoday.com.

54. Quoted in Aaron Tooley, "Interview with Dr. Jonathan B. Singer on Cyberbullying," *Online MSW Programs*, n.d. www.onlinemswprograms.com.

55. Jane Wakefield, "Is Your Child a Cyberbully and If So, What Should You Do?" *BBC*, January 6, 2017. www.bbc.com.

56. "Former Bullies Share What Motivated Behavior," *NPR*, March 23, 2010. www.npr.org.

57. "10 Steps to Stop and Prevent Bullying," *National Education Association*, n.d. www.nea.org.

58. Izzy Kalman, "Why Telling on Bullies Backfires," *Psychology Today*, May 30, 2014. www.psychologytoday.com.

FOR FURTHER RESEARCH

BOOKS

Emily Bazelon, *Sticks and Stones: Defeating the Culture of Bullying and Rediscovering the Power of Character and Empathy*. New York: Random House, 2013.

Lori Hile, *Bullying*. Chicago, IL: Heinemann Library, 2013.

Nick Hunter, *Cyber Bullying*. Chicago, IL: Heinemann Library, 2012.

Lester L. Laminack, *Bullying Hurts: Teaching Kindness Through Read Alouds and Guided Conversations*. Portsmouth, NH: Heinemann, 2012.

Aija Mayrock, *The Survival Guide to Bullying*. New York: Scholastic, 2015.

INTERNET SOURCES

Ulrich Boser, "How to Stop Bullying in Schools," *U.S. News and World Report*, February 27, 2018. www.usnews.com.

Eric Haseltine, "How to Stop Bullying (and Why People Don't Try It)," *Psychology Today*, October 20, 2017. www.psychologytoday.com.

"When Teasing Becomes Bullying," *Scholastic*, n.d. www.scholastic.com.

WEBSITES

American Psychological Association

www.apa.org

The American Psychology Association promotes psychology and how it can help society.

PACER's National Bullying Prevention Center

www.pacer.org

The National Bullying Prevention Center is an organization that helps prevent childhood bullying by providing resources and promoting social change.

Stomp Out Bullying

https://stompoutbullying.org

Stomp Out Bullying is an organization that works to reduce and prevent bullying and cyberbullying.

StopBullying.gov

www.stopbullying.gov

StopBullying.gov is an organization that provides tips for kids to identify bullying and teaches parents how they can prevent and stop bullying.

INDEX

Aitchison, Guy, 34
anti-bullying laws, 16, 57
art, 59–61
Attell, Brandon K., 48

Baltimore Sun, 60
Beckham, David, 27
Bennett, Tom, 39
Bottos, Lindsay, 59–61
Brady, Tom, 27
bullying and weight, 24, 52, 56
Burberry, 29
Byrne, MaryAnn, 9

Cecil the Lion, 32–34
Center for Psychological Studies, 11
Chemaly, Soraya, 41–42
Clementi, Jane, 21–22
Clementi, Tyler, 20–21
Columbine High School, 22
common targets of bullying, 38–53
Conan, Neal, 65
Cook, Jennifer, 47–48
Cross, Gail, 41
cyberbullying, 8, 10, 22, 36, 38, 40, 55–56, 60, 63

DeGeneres, Ellen, 56
domestic violence, 42
Douglas, Gabby, 24–25
Duff, Hilary, 27

Erwin, Michael, 50
European Anti-Bullying Network, 7, 8

Facebook, 12, 31, 36, 58, 66
Federal Bureau of Investigation (FBI), 14
Ford, Christine Blasey, 44–46
Freeman High School, 23

Georgia State University, 48
Grossman, Mallory, 6

Harris, Eric, 22
Hawkins, Natalie, 25
Houghton, Kristen, 54

Instagram, 12, 26–27, 58–59, 66

Jenkins, Nicola, 64
Jessica Logan Act, 16
Joe Shoemaker Elementary, 6

Kalman, Izzy, 68
Kamenetz, Anya, 23
Kavanaugh, Brett, 44
Konnikova, Maria, 8
Kotb, Hoda, 56

Lake Oswego High School, 47
Lawrence, Karma, 30, 31
Lensing, Molly, 28
LGBT community, 19–21, 49–50
Littleton, Colorado, 22
Logan, Cynthia, 15–16
Logan, Jessica, 15–17

76

Maryland Institute College of Art, 60
Meadows Ranch, 52
media, 22, 29, 44, 46, 66
Meier, Megan, 12–14
Meier, Tina, 14
minority groups, 48–50, 57
Mohammed, Farah, 37
Montgomery, Ohio, 15
Mosseri, Adam, 58–59
Myles, Jamel, 6
MySpace, 12, 14

National Domestic Violence Hotline, 42
National Education Association (NEA), 67
New England Journal of Medicine, 49
Nova Southeastern University, 11

Ontario, Canada, 35
Owens, Geoffrey, 30, 31

Palmer, Walter, 32–34
parent shaming, 26–30
Patterson, Susan, 8
people with disabilities, 50–53
Pepper, Penny, 52–53
Pew Research Center, 10, 43
physical abuse, 8, 38, 68
Pierce, Leia, 6
Poland, Scott, 11
prevention, 8, 16, 17, 18–19, 23, 48–50, 54–69
Prince William, 55–56
Psychology Today, 40, 62
punishing children through shaming, 35
Puth, Charlie, 56

Rutgers University, 20
Scheff, Sue, 35
Schorr, Melissa, 35
Schuster, Dr. Mark, 49
shaming businesses, 29
shaming cheaters, 35–37
Sharpe, Caleb, 23
Shields Middle School, 18
Singer, Dr. Jonathan B., 63
smartphones, 7, 14–15, 30
Smith, Mia, 47
Snapchat, 66
Stomp Out Bullying, 56
StopBullying.gov, 50, 57
suicide, 6–7, 8, 10, 13–14, 16–18, 20
Sycamore High School, 15

Temple University, 63
thredUP, 29
Today with Kathie Lee and Hoda, 26
Trader Joe's, 30
Trainor, Meghan, 26
Trump, Donald, 40, 44
Trump, Melania, 40
Tumblr, 60–61
Tyler Clementi Higher Education Anti-Harassment Act, 21

Union, Gabrielle, 27
University College Dublin, 34
US Supreme Court, 44

verbal abuse, 8
victims who bully others, 10, 22–23

INDEX CONTINUED

Whitson, Signe, 40, 62
Wickenburg, Arizona, 52
Williams, Lisa M., 19
Winter, Ariel, 25–26
Witsell, Donna, 18–19
Witsell, Hope, 17–18
workplace bullying, 8, 10, 48, 49, 50

Yale University, 16
Yannopoulos, Costas, 7, 8

Zuckerberg, Mark, 58

IMAGE CREDITS

Cover: © MachineHeadz/iStockphoto

4: © Tero Vesalainen/iStockphoto

5: © Leonard Zhukovsky/Shutterstock Images

7: © Ridofranz/iStockphoto

9: © Tero Vesalainen/iStockphoto

11: © Africa Studio/Shutterstock Images

13: © Deepak Sethi/iStockphoto

15: © Antonio Guillem/Shutterstock Images

21: © Mel Evans/AP Images

25: © Leonard Zhukovsky/Shutterstock Images

28: © Maria Sbytova/Shutterstock Images

33: © paula french/Shutterstock Images

39: © Daisy Daisy/Shutterstock Images

43: © Mladen Mitrinovic/Shutterstock Images

45: © Win McNamee/Abaca/Sipa USA/AP Images

51: © A_Lesik/Shutterstock Images

55: © SolStock/iStockphoto

57: © Red Line Editorial

59: © dolphfyn/Shutterstock Images

61: © Zabavna/Shutterstock Images

64: © David Pereiras/Shutterstock Images

68: © Monkey Business Images/Shutterstock Images

ABOUT THE AUTHOR

Tammy Gagne has written dozens of books for both adults and children. Her recent titles include *Pop Culture and Entertainment in the Twenty-First Century* and *Women in the Workplace*. She lives in northern New England with her husband, son, and a menagerie of pets.